Pepper™

THE PRESCHOOL PUPPY

in

The Call of the Ball

by:

GUY BROOKE

TATE PUBLISHING & *Enterprises*

YEPPER-DEPPER
HERE COMES
PEPPER!

Published by Tate Publishing & Enterprises, LLC
127 E. Trade Center Terrace | Mustang, Oklahoma 73064 USA
1.888.361.9473 | www.tatepublishing.com

Tate Publishing is committed to excellence in the publishing industry. The company reflects the philosophy established by the founders, based on Psalm 68:11,
"The Lord gave the word and great was the company of those who published it."

Book design copyright © 2008 by Tate Publishing, LLC. All rights reserved.
Cover design & interior design by Elizabeth A. Mason
Illustration by Kristen Polson

Published in the United States of America

ISBN: 978-1-60604-299-1
1. Juvenile Fiction: Animals: General: Ages 0-5
08.04.15

To Ashley and Tiffiny,

my two inspirations and the loves of my life.

Thank you, God, for daughters!

"Where's my ball?" Pepper the Preschool Puppy said with a yawn.

"It was right here last night, but now it's gone."

Up from his bed he jumped and he ran.

He just had to find his ball, and so the search began.

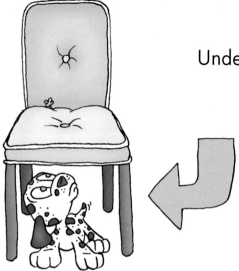

Under the chair? No, not there.

In the closet? No, not yet.

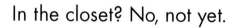

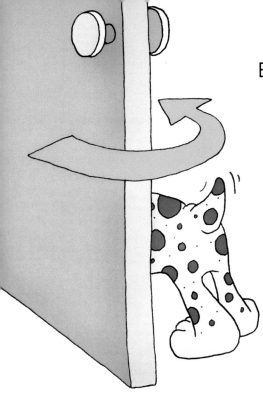

Behind the door? Oh, what a chore!

So he ran and he searched all over the floor.

"Hey, Skitty Kitty!" barked Pepper in a hurry,

which scared poor Skitty right out of his furry.

"Phift! Phift! Phift!" the old cat hissed,

which sounded like snakes when they

KISS   KISS

KISS.

"Was that you, puppy? You almost made me fall!"

"Yepper-depper, it's me, Pepper! Have you seen my ball?"

"Not again. No, not that!" cried the cat.

"Go away and don't be a pest. Can't you see? I'm trying to rest."

"My ball, my ball, my ball!" Pepper barked all the way out the door,

then he ran around the yard and barked and barked some more.

"Flutter–flutter–flutter!" came an answer to his cry.

Flutter-up, butter-up flew Buttercup the Butterfly.

"Flutter high,

flutter low,

I fluttered by to say, hello!"

On his nose she landed, straight and tall.

"Was that you, puppy, I heard call?"

"Yepper-depper, it was me, Pepper. Have you seen my ball?"

"Flutter me. . . flutter, oh my! Not this butterfly."

Then she spread her wings and softly waved goodbye.

"My ball. . . my ball. . . my ball. . ."
Pepper was feeling blue.

"I love to hear it crunch when I bite
down and chew,

and the jingle of the bell hidden
somewhere inside. . .

I WANT MY BALL!

Pepper the Preschool Puppy cried.

Back to the house, he sadly strolled in,

and there was Skitty Kitty, sleeping on the table again.

"Baaall?" Pepper slowly asked in a whisper,

but all he heard was,

PURRR   PURRR

PURRR

The sound was calm: PURRR... PURR...

The sound was sleepy: PURRR... PURR...

The sound made Pepper's eyes go dreamy.

"My bed, my bed. Must find my bed," he said,

then proceeded to lay down his sleepy little head.

JINGLE
JINGLE

came a sound from under the pillow.

His lost ball was calling to play,

but sleepy little Pepper was dreaming far, far away.

Yepper-depper, sweet dreams, Pepper,

for tomorrow's another day.

ARE YOU GOOD AT FINDING THINGS?

There are 12 hidden 4-leaf clovers in this book.

How many can you find?

Cut out this bookmark and
give it to a friend!

Let everyone know about

Pepper

THE PRESCHOOL PUPPY

The Call of the Ball, the first in a continuing series
of fun-loving stories about a fun-loving
puppy named Pepper.

SEE YOU NEXT TIME!

PEPPER THE
PRESCHOOL
PUPPY

The Call of
the Ball

by:
Guy Brooke

TATE PUBLISHING & *Enterprises*

www.tatepublishing.com/bookstore

888.361.9473

YEPPER-DEPPER
HERE COMES
PEPPER!